REBIRTH

FROM MY PAST

MARQUESSA PRATER

DEDICATION

"I would like to dedicate My Second Novella to My Favorite Girl in Heaven, My Grandmother Georgia W. Piedro A.K.A. Grama. If it wasn't for your encouragement, prayers, and love growing up, I don't think I would have made it this far to write, not one, but two books."
"You were My Number 1 Supporter then and you are still now. I feel your presence all the time. Thank you for keeping me going. We did it again. I love you forever!"

CONTENTS

ACKNOWLEDGMENTS

'I would like to take the time out to give thanks to God; I face many daring times and felt like stopping in this race. You wanted me to finish this race for the second round. You saw my purpose and wanted me to continue to share with the world. Thank you to My Hair Stylist, Makeup Artist, Book Designer and Photographer. Everyone did a phenomenal job. Thank you to everyone who purchases my book in person or online. Last but certainly not least, The Author of Rebirth from My Past, Marquessa Prater. I'm so proud of myself; it was a lot of rest stops, but I kept the faith and kept my trust in God and finished this race.

CHAPTER 1

Congratulations Tesla

Man, I miss you big guy; I'm seating on my bed, looking at daddy's picture, wishing he could be here. Today is my graduation day. A part of me is broken and happy at the same time. Since daddy's passing, Mama, Cedes and I have all tried to stay strong and keep his legacy alive.

Cedes: "Hey Tesla what are you doing?"

Tesla: "Just looking at a picture of daddy wishing he was here."

Cedes: "He is, sis and we are too, remember, whenever you need to talk, cry or laugh, I'm always here for you sis. I love you and am very proud of you. You could have made bad decisions but you didn't. In the mix of all the drama that went on in our home, not attending your Senior Prom, Your boyfriend being incarcerated, the loss of daddy, you continued to remain humble passing all your final exams. Sis "I admire you" I'm going to be your Biggest Cheerleader especially in the stands screaming your name today as you receive your diploma."

Tesla: "Aww! Thank you sis I love you so much."

Cedes: "I have something for you I think this is the perfect time for you to open it."

Tesla: Cedes, this is absolutely beautiful: I always wanted a locket but pink diamonds set it off. This gift is really nice. I will always cherish this gift. Give me some love sister."

Cedes: "OK, OK enough of that open the locket."

Tesla: "Cedes! Look at us all together again I love it, thank you."

Cedes: "Just know we are all we got and daddy is still here with us, not by sight but in spirit. Come on let's go downstairs, all the family members are here."

As Cedes and I began to walk downstairs, the family shouted "SURPRISE" as I reached the final steps. The living room was decorated with a Congratulations Banner that read, "Congratulations Telsa Class of 2021" with my picture on it. Mama had the tables and chairs decorated with Maroon and Gold, my school colors. Centerpieces were different pictures of me from then to now. Mama outdid herself with ice sculptures of a princess crown. We had food out of this world and the dessert table was to die for. My heart was so overjoyed. Even at our lowest moments, Mama still made a way. I will forever cherish this moment.

Diamond: "Look at my baby, you did it. I can't wait to see and hear them call your name across the stage."

Tesla: "No Mama! We did it, thank you so much for your encouragement and prayers through my journey. Thank you for always being there. Most importantly, thank you for being my mother. "I love you, "

Diamond: "Awww baby girl, thank you for such heartfelt words. You're always my baby. I'm extremely proud of you and your accomplishments; you deserve it."

Tesla: "Let me go upstairs and get my cap and gown."
Diamond: "I already have it down here, let me help you put it on. "Oops hat drop"

Tesla: "I'll get it Mama! You are about to make me cry again, look at daddy. Awww mama, how did you? When did you?

Diamond: "Don't worry about that (smiling) Look inside."

Tesla: Inside the hat, it read **"I walk with you across the stage and forever in my heart."**

"Thank you so much mama, I love you so much. Everything was starting to go better for me. I got on the steps to grab everyone's attention. I would like to thank you, everyone, for coming; this really meant a lot. Your support will never go unnoticed; thank you."

Diamond: "Okay everyone, let's start heading out, we have a Graduation to attend."

My family and I loaded up in the Mercedes Benz Party Bus talking, laughing having a good time. When we arrived at the graduation, I departed from everyone to be with My Graduation Class. As we prepare to line up in alphabetical order and began to walk out to our seats, I started to reflect on how My Senior Year was interrupted by the loss of my father and the incarceration of Rayquan. Our relationship is still growing strong. They haven't given him a court date. Every time he appears in court they adjourn the matter. Rayquan has been keeping me focused and all always makes me smile even behind bars. I wish I could share this moment with him; he deserves a proper thank you in person. I'm just going to make the best of it. My heart is beating fast because Ms. Hart is at the Podium.

"Dear Lord; I come to you again, please don't let Ms. Hart say a speech or call My Senior Class Names to receive Our Diploma. I've been through enough this year. She talks at a slow pace and we will be here forever. This is a celebration, not another day in class; fix it Jesus; Amen."

Principal Ross: "Good Afternoon everyone, I'm Principal Ross. Thank you all for coming to celebrate with Roosevelt Seniors today. Our High School Seniors will all go their separate ways as they enter New Journeys, New Careers and New Lifestyles."

Tesla: "God is definitely on time because Ms. Hart will not be speaking, Principal Ross and our Valedictorians are giving great speeches. Ok, they are about to call names; they are at the letter N. Mr. Wells is walking to our seats so we can line up to go on stage. Ok, my name is about to be called. Tesla Oakwood "here it goes." As I walk across the stage, I hear my name encore "Tesla!!!" The voice sounds familiar. I shook Mr. Ross' hand and continued to walk across the stage. As I snapped my photo, walking back to my seat, I still hear the voice still calling, "Tesla!!!" There was this man running down the bleachers with flowers covering his face. The flowers vanished from his face giving me a clearer vision. It was Rayquan. As the faculties at Roosevelt High are almost to the conclusion of calling the last couple of seniors' names, I shed tears of joy, My Best Friends and I made it. "I'm so proud of us." We all did it for someone this year. Cha-Cha did it for her Baby Girl Star. Destiny did it for her Big Mama & Lil Zack "Baby Brother. I did it for My Family & Rayquan. "I have been through a lot the last couple of months, but I kept my head up and walked by faith. Everything is starting to fall in place. This starts a New Chapter of My Life. I will face many obstacles, many trail and errors. "I couldn't do this without You, God. Principal Ross is walking to the podium, "It was a pleasure to be your Principal at Roosevelt High; I wish you all a beautiful journey; everyone will always be a part of me and if you ever feel alone, this will always be your home. I now present to you The Class of 2021." Everyone tossed their hats, hugging one another. I immediately ran to Cha-Cha and Destiny and said, "We did it". All of us were so happy. We immediately went to the back to get Our Diplomas.

Destiny: "Let me go find Big Mama and Lil Zack."

Cha-Cha: "I can't wait to kiss Star."

Tesla: "Yeah, let me go find mama and the rest of the family. Meet me back at my house. Mama throwing me a Graduation Party."

My Girls: "Ok we will be there soon!"

CHAPTER 2

"WE are so proud of you"

My Family: "Congratulations Tesla! We are so proud of you." I had so many Flowers, Balloons and Gifts.

        Diamond: "God, I thank You, as a Teenager Mother, I didn't know how I was going to do it with two babies, but by Your grace and mercy, I was able to finish with the help of their Father. Now, I have seen both of My Daughters walk across the stage to receive their Diplomas. I just want to thank You over and over again."

Tesla: "Thank you so much everyone for your support. Let's capture this moment; everyone get in let's take a photo." As the photographer was about to take the picture, Rayquan walked up; This photo wouldn't be complete without this gentleman. I walked over to grab Rayquan's hand. I could hear my family whispering, "Who is that?"

"Family, I have someone for you'll to meet; this handsome man is my Boyfriend, Rayquan."

Rayquan: "Hello everyone Nice to meet you'll."

Tesla: "Sorry to keep you waiting but it's a must my baby gets in this photo." The Photographer snapped the photo; I instantly know it was picture perfect. "Mama and Cedes this is Rayquan."

Rayquan: "Nice to meet the both of you, I heard so much about the both of you. My condolences continue to go out to each of you."

Diamond: "What an honor to finally meet you. Thank you so much for uplifting my baby's sprints. "Meeting my husband in jail, making him realize what was important and descent, turned his life around once he was released. I know this is not the way you picture it. Please accept this moment. I receive you with open arms to our family. Welcome Home!"

Cedes: "Thank you for everything, it's nice to finally put a face with a name. As long as you keep my Baby Sister happy, I'm happy."

Rayquan: "I'm very pleased to meet all of you. I am finally getting to make things right with my baby. I promise I will always be here for all of you. Just like Dollar and Tesla were here for me. I used to look at life differently until I met both of them. The streets are not for me anymore. I started a Barber School in two weeks and soon I will have a Barber Shop. I assure Dollar I was leaving the streets alone. He paid a way for me, another chance at life and I will make him proud. This lovely beautiful young lady showed me what I was missing in a woman. If it is ok with you Mrs. Oakwood, I would like to present your daughter with this ring."

Diamond: "It's alright with me"

Tesla: "Oh my God! This ring is absolutely gorgeous."

Rayquan: "It's not an Engagement Ring, soon it will be. This is a Promise Ring to show you that you're the only person I see myself with. Soon this ring will be upgraded to an Engagement Ring. Tesla, you have changed my life for the better."

Tesla: "Aww baby, thank you so much and you're the only man for me." I lean over to hug and kiss Rayquan. He really gives me butterflies and this is the stomachache I don't mind having. I want this love forever." After Graduation, we all headed back to my house to celebrate with all my family and friends. Everyone is having a good time. "Man this food from Grama is good huh?"

Cha-Cha: "Yes it really is" (smiles)

Dwayne: "Where are my manners? I'm too busy trying to eat. I apologize; Hello, my name and is Dwayne. I'm Tesla's Cousin. Who might this beautiful young lady standing next to me be?"

Cha-Cha: "Hi my name is Chasity, but prefers to be called Cha-Cha. I'm Tesla's Best Friend."

Dwayne: "Oh WOW! It's a pleasure to meet you and congratulations to you as well."

Cha-Cha: "Thank you"

Dwayne: "Come on grab a plate let's sit and chat. So what are your plans now that you completed High School?"

Cha-Cha: "Well, I plan on attending college and finding a good job with benefits to provide for my daughter and myself.

Dwayne: "That sounds like you have your head in the right direction. You mentioned daughter, how old is she?"

Cha-Cha: "She is 1, Star is my pride and joy. I do it all for her.

Dwayne: "I like that, I'm really enjoying our conversation; I would like to talk with you more. That's if you don't have a man.

Cha-Cha: "How old are you?"

Dwayne: I'm 28, I tell you what, here is my business card. I own Dripping Auto & Paint Shop off of Prater & 18th. Anytime you need your car painted or service, everything is on me. Considered it as a Graduation Gift."

Cha-Cha: "Thank you I will need a car first."

Dwayne: "It's one coming, I'm going to let you continue to enjoy yourself. It was nice talking to you. Hopefully, you will put my business card to use."

Cha-Cha: "It was nice talking with you as well and I just might hold you to that. Have a good rest of night."

Destiny: "Girl, I saw you over there giggling and stuff with his fine ass. That's Tesla's Cousin, Right?"

Cha-Cha: "Yes that's him"

"Can I have everyone's attention? Thank you everyone for coming out to celebrate with me. Mama thank you for putting this all together, Everything looks nice and everyone looks great.

I couldn't ask for a better day. Thank you. now let's enjoy ourselves"

CHAPTER 3

"LITTLE black dress"

I s this how it feels to be a graduate? "No more alarm clocks going off early in the morning; Mama screaming my name to come and eat breakfast It's 10:00 am; I can't recall the last time I slept past 8:00 AM. Time to get my day started. Oh Wow!

Look at all these heartfelt text messages. It's too early to cry pull yourself together Tesla. There is nothing like support coming from Family and True Friends. I will never forget the talks, prayers, and words of wisdom. "Anytime I needed them, someone was there even before daddy passed. " Oh, I can't forget that Rayquan was there at the most difficult time in my life. He found ways to call me Morning, Noon and Night. He made sure I wasn't late for school, ate breakfast before my final exams and prayed for me. We finish this together I couldn't ask for a Better Man. Speaking of him, he's calling now.

Rayquan: "Good Morning, Beautiful; how are you?"

Tesla: "Good Morning, Handsome; great now I'm talking to you. How are you?"

Rayquan: "Great! I wanted to know if I can make it up to you and take you out tonight?"

Tesla: "Of course you can, but you already have in so many ways."

Rayquan: "Well it's a date at 7 pm. I can't wait to see you."

Tesla: "I can't wait to see you too baby; see you soon. (Called Ended)

I'm about to pull out My Black Balenciaga Dress; one-sleeve body wrap and My Balenciaga Wrap-Around Heels the same outfit. I was going to wear it on our initial first date. downstairs to the Beauty Bar and have Jada wand curl my hair and do my makeup like I had that same night. As I head back upstairs from getting doll up, I could hear music coming from my room."Avant: This is your night" and that's exactly what it was. I lighted my candles and turned up the music. As I turned the showerhead on I face the opposite direction towards the wall letting the water run down my back, my soap lathered on my washcloth as it connects on my body slowly. My hands made it around different parts of my body. The same way I want Rayquan to tough me. I began to clean my vagina as I release the washcloth from my hands and letting my finger work inside of me. I wanted to pre-plan how it feels to be tough sexually. Still slowly rocking and dancing to the music as my finger is still inserted in me; I'm about to climax. I pat dry my body off massage lotion over my entire body spraying my favorite fragrance, "Kurkdjian Baccarat Rouge 540." As I slip on my dress and heels released the pins from my hair, "I felt no longer like a Teenager Girl. Tonight, "I'm a Woman".

CHAPTER 4

"YOU give good love"

Rayquan: "Hey Baby,
I'm at your gate, can you let me in?"
Tesla: "Hey Baby! Okay.
I'm opening it now. I will be down shortly."

"Dear God; Let this be a good night, I finally found someone real, beautiful and accept me for me. Tesla never judges me. "Let tonight be special; remove all negative energy away from us in Jesus' name Amen. Let me get out of this car and ring the doorbell.

Diamond: "Hello Rayquan,"

you look handsome; how are you?"

Rayquan: "Hello Mrs. Oakwood"

I'm doing well, thanks for asking. "These flowers are for you. How have you been?"

Diamond: Thank you Rayquan, these flowers are absolutely beautiful and I've been good, can't complain; it's so good to see you."

Rayquan: "It's good to see you as well."

Diamond: "You take care of my baby and show her a nice time."

Rayquan: "Yes ma'am! I wouldn't have it any other way. Hello beautiful, you look absolutely gorgeous; these are for you.

Tesla: "Thank you baby, "so beautiful". Mama, I will be back soon.

Diamond: "You both look great to have a nice time."

Tesla: "Yes ma'am! We will."

Rayquan: "Let me get the door for my beautiful lady." **Tesla:** Thank you baby!"

Rayquan took me to Pier called Sunset; it was the perfect name, absolutely breathtaking. We sat, talked, and grabbed Butter Pecan Ice Cream at this Ice cream Parlor named Scoops. Rayquan told me how this spot was special to him. His parents used to take him here every Friday after school when he was little and get ice cream at the same ice cream parlor. After we finished with our ice, Rayquan let me know he had a couple of more surprises for me but since I have heels on, he had a Biker ride us to the other location. He said he couldn't have his lady feet hurting. He always says the sweetest things and continues to make me smile. As we rode through a neighborhood in the Heights, He pointed the house he was raised in to me. At the end of the block was the Church he used to attend. We stopped at the light, it was this lady selling glow-in-the-dark roses. He brought all 12 to make me a dozen red roses.

Tesla "Baby, you are giving me Butterflies. This is by far the sweetest date."

Rayquan: "You haven't seen anything yet baby," Bossman, we will get off from here. We are not too far from where we parked. **Tesla:** "Thank you for such great hospitality; we had a great time."

Rayquan: "Please keep the change."

Tesla: "Ok baby."

Rayquan: "I have this nice restaurant that I want to take you to. It's in the hood but the food is great!"

Tesla: "That's fine baby, I'm enjoying my time with you and I know you wouldn't let anything happen to me." We pulled up to this place I'm looking like I'm to dress up but kept it cute. "I'm like Tesla, don't mess up a good night for the appearance of a building." When we approach the door, Rayquan has full access to the building. As we walk in, it was a whole candlelight dinner waiting for both of us and only him and me.

Rayquan: "Tesla you mean a lot to me. I obey what Dollar asks me to do and that's to attend Barber School. "Now I'm a Certified Barber and now owner; this is our building. We are sitting and having dinner in our New Shop. "I'm naming the shop Dollars."

Tesla: "Oh my goodness! I'm so proud of you and daddy is too. I know he's smiling in Heaven. You went out of your way to plan all this; I have never experienced this type of love; only from my parents. Everything was beautiful.

Rayquan: "Tesla, look at me I'm stopping it all for us. I want to become a Better Man. I never would've thought I would have my own shop. No one ever gave me unconditional love like you and your family did. I never knew how to love until I met you.

This is Our Shop. We will make love in this shop, pray in this shop, and make money in this shop."

Rayquan reached out and began kissing me, singing in my ear; Remarkable by Jahiem. Feeding me chocolate covered with strawberries. R& B Slow Jams began to play in the background, setting the mood right. "We walked backwards towards the wall still kissing, hugging and touching each other. Whitney Houston's "You Give Good Love" began to play as Rayquan started slowly undressing me while his lips work their way over my entire body. He began to give me oral and licking the chocolate off my body. I'm ripping his shirt as soon as he made his way back up to me. We walk over to the couch. Rayquan laid me back on the couch and started to insert his penis into my vagina slowly still kissing me. "He took his time with me. It wasn't rushed, it was perfect and my cherry just popped.

CHAPTER 5

"DOLLAR'S is officially OPEN"

"We want to thank everyone for coming to our Grand Opening. May I ask that everyone bows your heads in a short prayer." "Dear Lord, I ask for Your graceful guidance as we build and grow this Business. We put our trust in Your hands that You will bless Our Business, Our Suppliers, Our Customers, and Our Employees.

We pray that You protect this business and the investments we put into it in Jesus' name Amen." "Before we cut the ribbon, may I ask for a moment of silence for Dollar, My Parents and Grandmother. Nothing would've been possible without them and if they were here, I know they all will be front and center." Good Afternoon everyone, for the ones that might not know me, my name is Tesla Oakwood (girlfriend) of this New Owner.

Rayquan: "Excuse me Baby! "May I add something to your speech?

Tesla: Sure!

Rayquan: "Soon will be my Wife "Ladies and Gentlemen".

Crowd: "Aww I know that's right" (clapping hands).

Tesla: Aww Baby (smiling) "Thanks to everyone for taking the time out of your business schedule. This accomplishment was very important to Rayquan; the fact he included me in His Business. My heart is overjoyed; his love for others is indescribable. He taught me "just because the race gets hard never quit." He was determined and everyone here gets to witness what determination gets you. I'm extremely proud of you."

Rayquan: Thank you Baby and for being My Number One Supporter "I love you" (embraces Tesla with love) Could our New Employees could come up? I would like everyone to meet our new barbers, Big Dot and Manny. "I have seen our barbers work. What an honor to have both of you working with us. I can't wait to experience all the laughter and amazing work of art of transformation for each customer. With that being said, scissors please! On the count of three, everyone will say Dollars. 123!!! DOLLARS. Welcome everyone, we are officially open for business; come inside. "Everyone please help yourself to refreshments; don't forget to sign The Wall of Fame. Who's ready for a Dollar Cut?

Ounce: "Oh so that's how we do Quan?

Rayquan: "Ounce, leave if you're going to cause a scene." **Ounce**: "Oh so you will kick me out after all we have been through?

Rayquan: "Yes if that's what it takes this is a happy moment for me and as a friend, you should be happy not disrespecting our shop.

Ounce: "Our shop? "I know you and that whore didn't open a shop?

Rayquan: "Look I said you will not disrespect our shop, My Lady or my happiness; now leave. I'm done with the streets. This is my new opportunity for a better life.

Ounce: "You so fuck up about this bitch. You did turn Godly and shit! Who the fuck are you?

Rayquan: "Not my past" Now leave!

Ounce: "Yeah I'll see you around better watch your back.
Rayquan: "NO! WATCH YOURS.

Later on D-Block "Who is that in that Black F150?"

Anonymous Driver: Aye! "You saw Quan?

Ounce: NO! "He left the block for that weak ass shop and following that weak ass bitch every move. I don't fuck with him anymore."

Anonymous Driver: "Damn! Aye, you got a lighter?

Ounce: "Yea hold up."

Anonymous Driver: NO! "You hold up. That weak bitch is my niece. I saw how you disrespect them at their Grand Opening earlier and especially on My Best Friend Name. This is not your first time. Well, this is your LAST! *Gun Fire POW! (3x) who is the weak bitch now?" (Truck speeds off). Everyone took off running. BREAKING News a 35yrs old male has been gunned down on D-Block. He has been identified as Christopher Morris and alias name Ounce. "If anyone has seen or heard anything, please contact Crime Stoppers as we continue this investigation.

Rayquan: "Oh Shit!"

Tesla: "What happened baby?

Rayquan: "Someone just killed Ounce Damn Man!

"No matter what, we were like family. Damn Man! (Crying)

Tesla: "It's going to be alright baby; you did all you could do to be there for Ounce."God knows best. "I'm sorry this happened to him, I'm here for you baby, always."

CHAPTER 6

"if he's mines prove it"

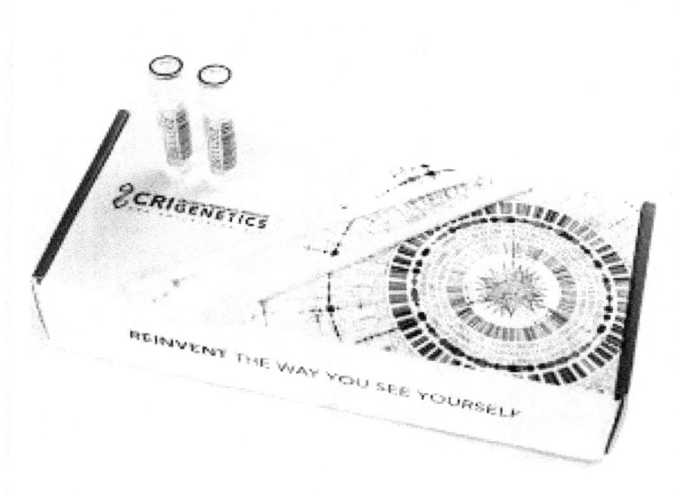

" A fter what happened to Ounce and seeing him in a casket, I'm glad I left the streets alone. The D-Block has been heavy with the Police ever since Ounce was murdered. They still haven't found who murdered

Ounce. "I hate to say it, but they don't really care. It is just another way to put another Drug Dealer in jail. I have my mind on the right track. Nothing or no one will get in the way of my happiness. Let me grab the keys and set the alarm."

Anonymous Women: "Well, well, look what we have here! Oh, so you can open a shop and not take care of your son?"

Rayquan: La'Kisha, what are you talking about? I haven't seen, heard or been with you in 2yrs.

La'Kisha: "Yeah, the 2yrs you missed out in Rayquan Jr's life. Oh, that's about to change. This whole shop will be his soon. I promise you no good ass nigga.

Tesla: "Is everything okay baby?"

Rayquan: "Yeah! everything is fine."

La'Kisha: "Oh hell! Who the hell are you supposed to be Iyanla, Fix My Life?"

Tesla: "No but the name is Tesla and this man right here is part of my life. You were saying?"

La'Kisha:" I was saying he needs to take care of his damn baby.

Tesla: "He will take a DNA Test. We will not be taking care of any baby unless it's ours. We will get in touch with you when the test results come in.

La'Kisha: Bitch BYE!

Tesla: "I'll be that.

Rayquan: "Soon as I start to be on the right path, here goes the enemy trying to still my joy.

Tesla: "They won't win baby! We are a team, I got you like you got me. If you are the father, I'm still going to be right beside you., helping take care of Rayquan Jr. If La'Kisha thought we were going to split up because of this, she is a damn lier. We all have a past and she was in the picture before me. So how can I get mad at you?"

Rayquan: "See, this is why I love you; you're so different. Tesla, most women would have left."

Tesla: "I'm not them Let's go take this DNA Test.

Clerk: "Good Afternoon welcome to DNA 100% Test Results. How may I help you?"

Rayquan: "Good Afternoon, my name is Rayquan Morehouse, I'm here to take a DNA Test.

Clerk: "I will need two forms of Identification for you to fill out this information. Someone will call you to the back shortly Mr. Morehouse."

Rayquan: "Okay! Thank you."

Clerk: "Ok you're all set Mr. Morehouse Expect your results back in two weeks. Have a nice day!"

"Today is the day the test results are in. I can't wait any longer. "When it comes to Rayquan Morehouse Jr Rayquan Morehouse. You are NOT the Father."

CHAPTER 7

"Let them play while we talk"

Big Dot: "Why are you looking so mean?"

     Destiny: "Go on Big Dot I'm not messing with anybody, just minding my business, waiting on Tesla and Cha-Cha.

    Big Dot: "I want to make you my business but am scared to say something. You look like you would hurt somebody."

Destiny: "Well you judging me for no reason."

Big Dot: "I'm just messing with you." I have been feeling you and want to know if I can take you out?

Destiny: "I'm not gay"

Big Dot: "See, you are judging me; I was just talking about hanging out. I overheard you have a little brother. He is the same age as my little brother Cody. I'm spending time with him Friday and he wanted to go to Dave & Buster's. I thought you would like to come. Maybe I can beat you in a smile (laughing)

Destiny: "See you got jokes but we can use a night out. Okay! It's a date see you Friday at 6 pm. I can pick both of you up if you like."

Destiny: "Okay! Here is my address."

Tesla: "Hey girl!" Are you ready to go?"

Destiny: "It's about time, where is Cha-Cha?"

Tesla: "Star doesn't feel good; she is in for the night.

Destiny: "Ok let's go! I'm starving."

Tesla: "See you later Big Dot"

Big Dot: "Okay Boss Lady! "Bye mean ass" (Laughing).

Destiny: "Bye!"

Big Dot: "Hey Mean Ass; excuse Me!" "My apologies Destiny. What are you laughing at? Get in and you must be Zack?"

Zack: "Yes!

Big Dot: "Nice to meet you. My name is Big Dot and this is my little brother Cody. "What's up man? (Handshake in the back seat) Aye Cody, this Zack meet Big Sister Destiny. Destiny (turn around)

Destiny: Hello, nice to meet you too ma'am. Nice to meet you as well Cody.

"We headed to Dave & Buster's. The boys act like they have known each other for a long time. Thank you Big Dot for inviting us. "I haven't seen my brother smile like this since my mother died. "It's been hard you know. I hide a lot of my hurt because I have to be strong for Zack. "You ever feel alone? Yes but you're not alone anymore you have a new friend now. Oh shit! Is that a smile? Wow!!!"You're already fine but drop-dead gorgeous when you smile. "I would like to take you out again if that's ok? "Sure I'll like that." Zack and Cody come and eat. Zack and Cody running to the table out of breath. "Man this so much fun thanks guys. "You're welcome!

CHAPTER 8

"I found what i been missing"

C hasity: Hello! Hi Dwayne, This is Chasity Tesla's best friend.

Dwayne: Wow! "I'm happy to hear your voice and glad you called. I thought about you for quite some time now. How have you and Star been?"

Chasity: "We have been well. How have you been?

Dwayne: "I have no complaints.

Chasity: "I'm happy to hear that. You mentioned that you have been thinking about me. Well, I have been thinking about you too and haven't stopped. Thank you for the words of encouragement. Today I enroll myself in Nursing School and they are paying everything in full at the Neighborhood Service Center plus Star Daycare. I know God heard my cry."

Dwayne: "I'm so happy for you and Star. I'm here to help you in any way I can. What are you doing tomorrow?"

Chasity: "Nothing plan at the moment."

.Dwayne: "I would like to take you and Star out and get to know both of you.

Chasity: We will like that Dwayne: tomorrow it's a date.

Dwayne: "I will pick you both up at 12:00 pm. I will call you when I'm on the way to send me your address.

Chasity: "Sounds great! See you soon! (Called ended)

Destiny: "Meanwhile thank you Big Dot for dropping us off.

Big Dot: "No problem at all."

Destiny: "See you later Big Dot. Later Lil Zack, be good in school.

Lil Zack: "Okay, I will."

Big Dot: Hold up Destiny let me talk to you for a minute. "Look, I've been enjoying the vibe lately. We have been talking about a lot of stuff. I haven't even told my own family. " I know you are not gay or anything.

Destiny: "Be quiet Big Dot and kiss me. Well damn!

Big Dot: "You shut me up (Laughing).

"I never thought I could vibe on a personal level only from best friends. You showed me different; I no longer care what anyone thinks about me switching over. You care for me. You care about me leveling up the right way instead of shaking my ass,

Destiny: "You love my little brother and he loves you. I want this and I'm ready to make it official with your gay ass. "Kiss me again and let me know it's real.

"Kissing"

"Oh yeah! It's definitely chemistry in Chevy. Call me later Dot"

Big Dot: "Will do."

Destiny: Damn! Are you calling now

Big Dot: "The way I feel about you I don't waste time." See you later. "

CHAPTER 9

"I want this forever"

"Time to head out to the Men Empowerment Event that Rayquan, My Cousin Dwayne and Uncle Tunk are hosting at Garden Park. "Rayquan is providing Free Haircuts, Dwayne is giving a $1000 Check from his Paint Shop Dripping to a High School Graduate that enters Dripping Contest. "Who will be attending Auto Body Program at Bobs Technical Center in The Fall.? "My Uncle Tunk provided all the Water Slides and Bounce Houses from His Business A&E. "Grama provided all the food. So many people donated Clothes, Shoes, School and Supplies. "They did it so big. Even Sunshine Energy sponsored to pay 100 Low Income Households Electricity for 2months. "I'm so proud of my family and man. "Hello everyone, my name is Rayquan. "I'm the Owner of Dollars Cuts. Thank you all for coming out to Our Men Empowerment Event. We didn't expect to see over 500 people out here. All I can say is WOW! We are truly thankful. I'm going to pass the microphone over to the other two men in charge of this event. I'll be back shortly to close out."

"Hello everyone, my name is Dwayne; I'm the Owner of Dripping Paint Shop. I won't hold everyone long but I will say go after your dreams and since we are going after our dreams, I would like to present this check of $1000 from Dripping Paint Shop to Charles Allen to go towards his Tuition at Bobs Technical Center in The Fall Congratulations. (Everyone clapping).

"Hello! My name is Tunk, Owner of A& E Bounce Houses & Waterslides. I never thought this day would come. I would stop selling Drugs and turn my life over to Christ and do something positive with the community. Change won't happen overnight. Keep the faith and your trust in Him. It can happen. Thank you all for coming out to our 1st Annual Event and this definitely won't be our last; God Bless. Now I will turn the microphone over to Rayquan.

"Like all two men, just stay focused and keep your eye on what you want to become and don't give up. It takes a lot of time to trust and love again. I didn't know how to love because I have never been loved but all that changed when I met the Oakwoods. Bernie Oakwood A.K.A Dollar changed my life for the better. Even though he has transitioned with the Lord, I have his family and madly in love with his daughter Tesla. I ask that Tesla come to the stage. "Tesla, I couldn't go on without you." I would like to know, would you?" "Excuse me everyone," the Helicopter was so loud I let it go by before I finished what I was saying. Everyone started clapping and smiling reading what's in the sky. Tesla turns to me crying, "Yes Baby! YES!"

CHAPTER 10

"IT'S a boy!

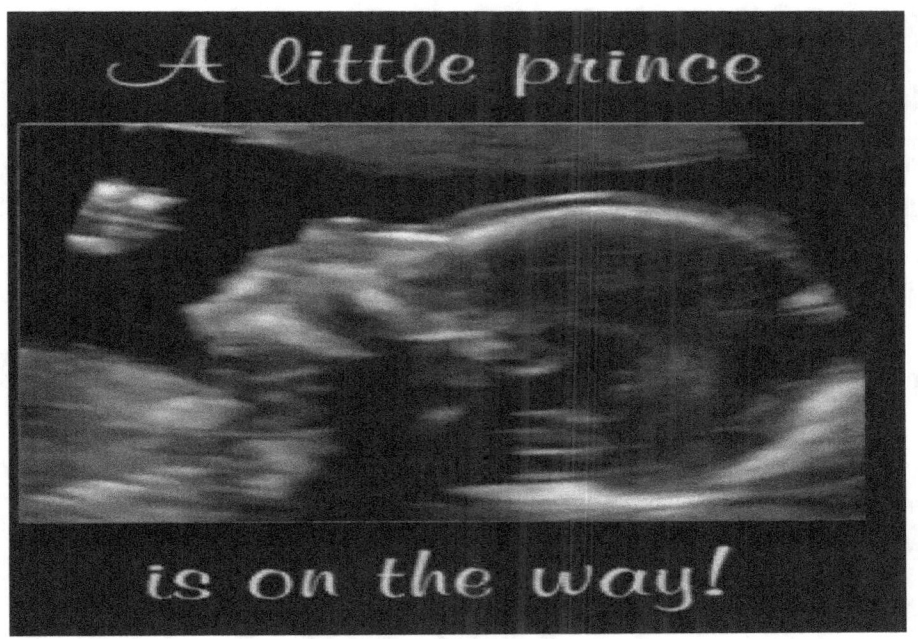

"Ok Ms. Oakwood, it's safe to say you will be a mommy very soon." "Oh my goodness, I never thought I will be a mommy (crying) looking at Rayquan while he was full of excitement. "I know the both of you will be great first-time parents. See you in a couple of weeks to find out the sex of the baby." Everyone was ecstatic soon as they found out. My mom and Cedes started ordering all kinds of stuff and don't even know the sex of the baby. Cha-Cha and Destiny fighting over being God Parents which they both are I just haven't told them yet. My family is so excited and Quan has been there for me making sure I'm comfortable, ate, etc. "I couldn't ask for a better man. As weeks went by, Rayquan and I found out the sex of the baby. We are expecting a boy. We are so excited to meet Our Baby Boy. "Mama, Cedes, Destiny and Cha-Cha gave Rayquan and me the best outdoor baby shower we could have imagined.

Top tier everything from the food cake, and decor. So many family and friends came out. Quan got to meet his father's and mother's families. He hasn't seen anyone since he was 15yrs old; since his parents passed away. "He was so emotional but happy at the same time. "I know he will cherish this moment forever. It feels good to see him happy especially at a perfect time; Rayquan Jr will arrive any day now. I don't know how they did it but they did." You had to be there to witness. It was definitely love in the room. Later that day, we went back to our house and set up Rayquan Jr's Nursery and packed our bags for the hospital. Around 10:18 pm my water broke. Quan got everything and rushed us to the hospital. When we arrived at the hospital, the Nurses and Doctors asked I wanted any medication to calm down the pain. I refused; I wanted to experience the pain; I didn't want anything to harm our baby. I began to push at 8:15 am. We welcome our baby boy at 7lbs 6oz. I shed tears of joy. The Nurses cleaned Rayquan Jr up and passed him over to Rayquan. I was too weak to hold him. Rayquan set in the chair and began talking to Rayquan Jr." "I did it all for Your Mother; now all for you Son. Thank you for changing me into a Better Man. Today I was born again I'm rebirth from my past."

Book Cast Members

Bernie A.K.A. Dollar (The Father)

Diamond (The Mother)

Mercedes (Sister)

Tesla (Daughter & Main Character)

Rayquan (Tesla Boyfriend)

Cha-Cha & Destiny (Tesla Best Friends)

Ounce (Rayquan Homeboy)

Star (Cha-Cha Daughter)

Manny (New Barber)

Big Dot (New Barber)

Dwayne (Tesla Cousin)

Tunk (Tesla Uncle)

Cody (Big Dot Brother)

Big Mama (Destiny Grandmother)

Mr. Ross (Tesla Principal)

Ms. Hart (Tesla Teacher)

La'Kisha (Rayquan Ex-Girlfriend)

Jada (Beautician)